some racing cars

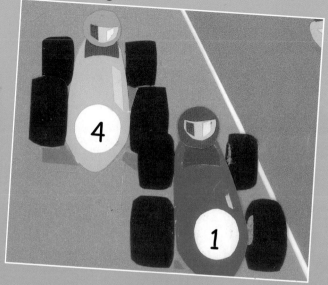

a bus stop

Using this book

Ladybird's *talkabouts* are ideal for encouraging children to talk about what they see. Bold colourful pictures and simple questions help to develop early learning skills – such as matching, counting and detailed observation.

Look at this book with your child. First talk about the pictures yourself, and point out things to look at. Let your child take his* time. With encouragement, he will start to join in, talking about the familiar things in the pictures. Help him to count objects, to look for things that match, and to talk about what is going on in the picture stories.

*To avoid the clumsy use of he/she, the child is referred to as 'he', **talkabouts** are suitable for both boys and girls.*

Published by Ladybird Books Ltd
80 Strand London WC2R ORL
A Penguin Company

1 3 5 7 9 10 8 6 4 2

© LADYBIRD BOOKS MMIII

Printed in Italy

talkabout

Cars

written by Lorraine Horsley
illustrated by Alex Ayliffe

Ladybird

Big cars, little cars
driving up the road!
Can you find these cars?

Which is your favourite car?

Find another...

racing car

taxi

van

How many red cars can you count altogether?

Pack up the car! It's time to go!
Tell the story.

On motorways you can drive quickly.
Where should you drive slowly?

We're all going on a journey.
Follow us...

up the hill...

down the hill...

vroom

chugga
chugga

past the sheep

over the bridge

bumpety   bump

12

round the corner

splish splash

screech!

through the puddle

and into the tunnel.

beep
beep

Can you make the car noises?

13

Vroom, vroom!
Racing cars, speeding for the line.
Who is in front and who is behind?

14

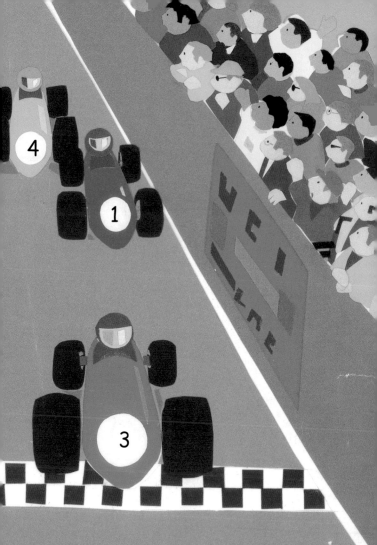

What colours are the cars?

Match each picture to its shadow.

The wheel is flat, the car won't go.
How would you fix it, do you know?

Point to the longest car.

How many people are in each car?
Do you like big cars or little cars?

What is happening at the petrol station?

What colour cars can you see?

Cars red and cars blue,
Count one, count two!
How many...

red cars

blue cars

yellow cars

green cars

orange cars?

Splish, splash! Bubble and foam.
Tell the story.

Can you find these things in the picture?

29

Can you find these as well?

some flowers

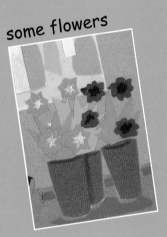

a traffic cone

some cows